This Little Tiger book belongs to:

_____

_____

_____

For Cameron, who loves stories
~ A M

For Miłosz and Mateusz
~ M B

LITTLE TIGER PRESS LTD,
an imprint of the Little Tiger Group
1 Coda Studios, 189 Munster Road,
London SW6 6AW
www.littletiger.co.uk
First published in Great Britain 2019
This edition published 2020

A CIP catalogue record for this book is available from the British Library
All rights reserved • ISBN 978-1-78881-381-5
Printed in China • LTP/1400/1338/0220
2 4 6 8 10 9 7 5 3 1

PiRATES DON'T GO TO SCHOOL!

Alan MacDonald

Magda Brol

LITTLE TIGER
LONDON

On the *Salty Prawn*, the pirates were busy.
"Swab the poop deck!" hollered Pa.
"Scrape them barnacles!" shouted Ma.
"Mend the mainsail!" cried Gran.
"And where's my tea, Jake?"
But Jake was tired of mopping parrot poop.
"Pa, when can I go to school?" he sighed.

"SCHOOL?" gasped his family. "Pirates don't go to school!"
"School is hard and horrible!" growled Pa.
"It's all rotten work and rotten rules," muttered Ma.
"And teachers is mean as sea monsters!" warned Gran.
But Jake longed to go and he kept on asking.

"All right, all right, we surrender!" groaned Pa. "YOU CAN GO TO BLOOMIN' SCHOOL!"

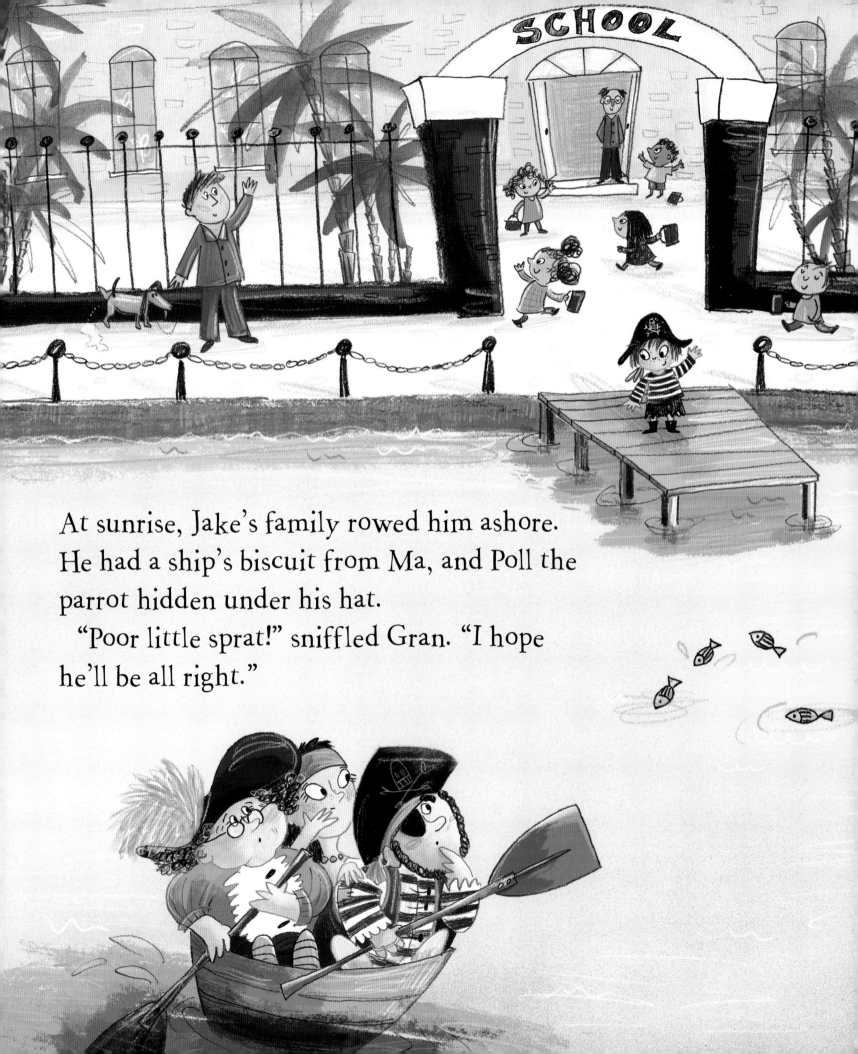

At sunrise, Jake's family rowed him ashore. He had a ship's biscuit from Ma, and Poll the parrot hidden under his hat.

"Poor little sprat!" sniffled Gran. "I hope he'll be all right."

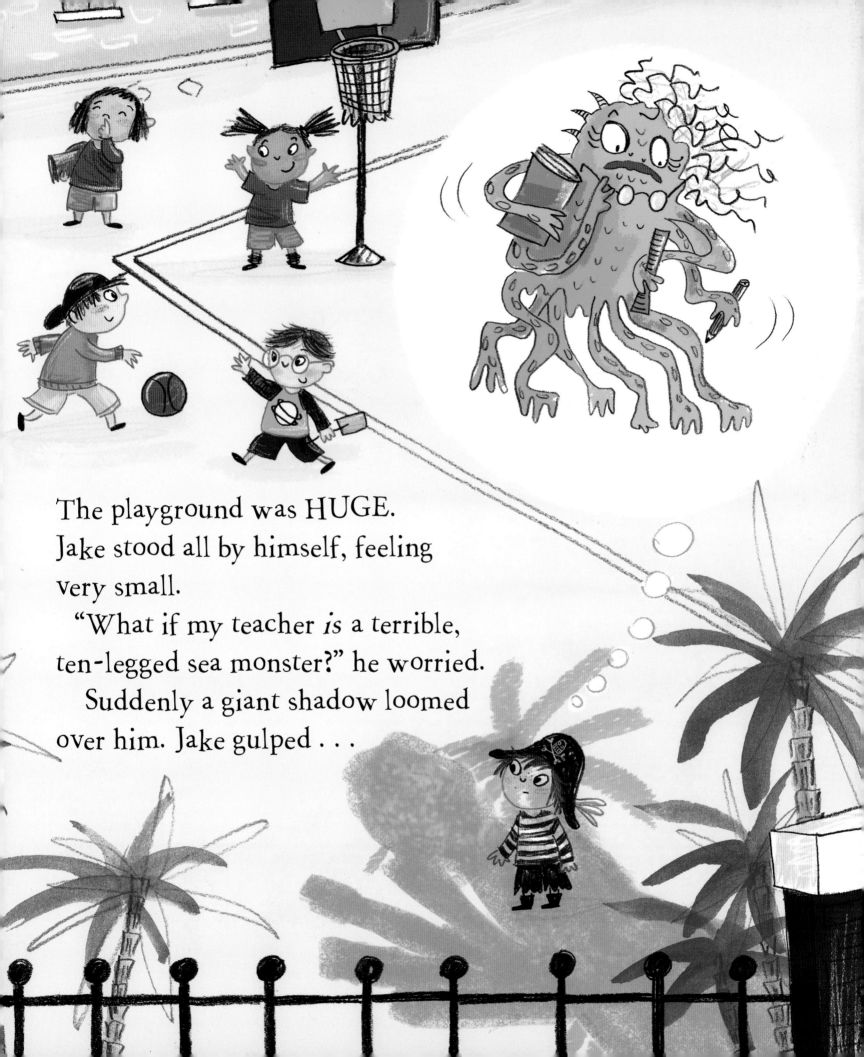

The playground was HUGE.
Jake stood all by himself, feeling
very small.

"What if my teacher *is* a terrible,
ten-legged sea monster?" he worried.

Suddenly a giant shadow loomed
over him. Jake gulped . . .

"You must be Jake,"
smiled Miss Cherry.
"Come and meet the
class!"

"Ahoy there, mates," said Jake,
raising his hat politely. But
he'd forgotten what was
underneath! Poll woke up
with a screech and took off.

ARK!

"Good heavens!" gasped Miss Cherry.
"Oh no!" cried Jake. "Come back,
you pesky parrot, come back!"

They chased Poll into the hall where
a gym lesson was in full swing.
"Heave-ho, mates," cried Jake.
"I've got her cornered."
Quick as a monkey, he climbed
up a rope. But Poll didn't
wait to be caught.

"Oh dear!" sighed Miss Cherry.
"Blow me down!" moaned Jake.

Outside, Jake hunted high and low.

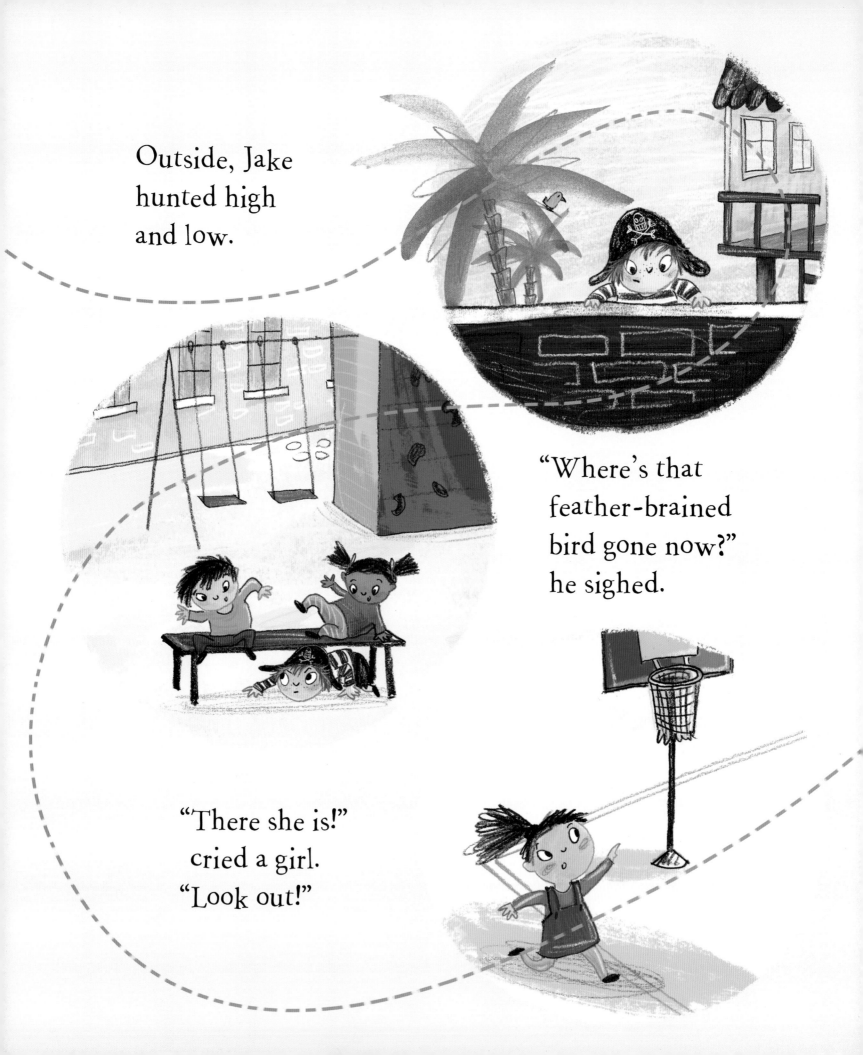

"Where's that feather-brained bird gone now?" he sighed.

"There she is!" cried a girl. "Look out!"

The headteacher hit the
deck as Poll swooped low
across the playground.
"Sink me!" groaned
Jake. "What now?"

But then he
had an idea!

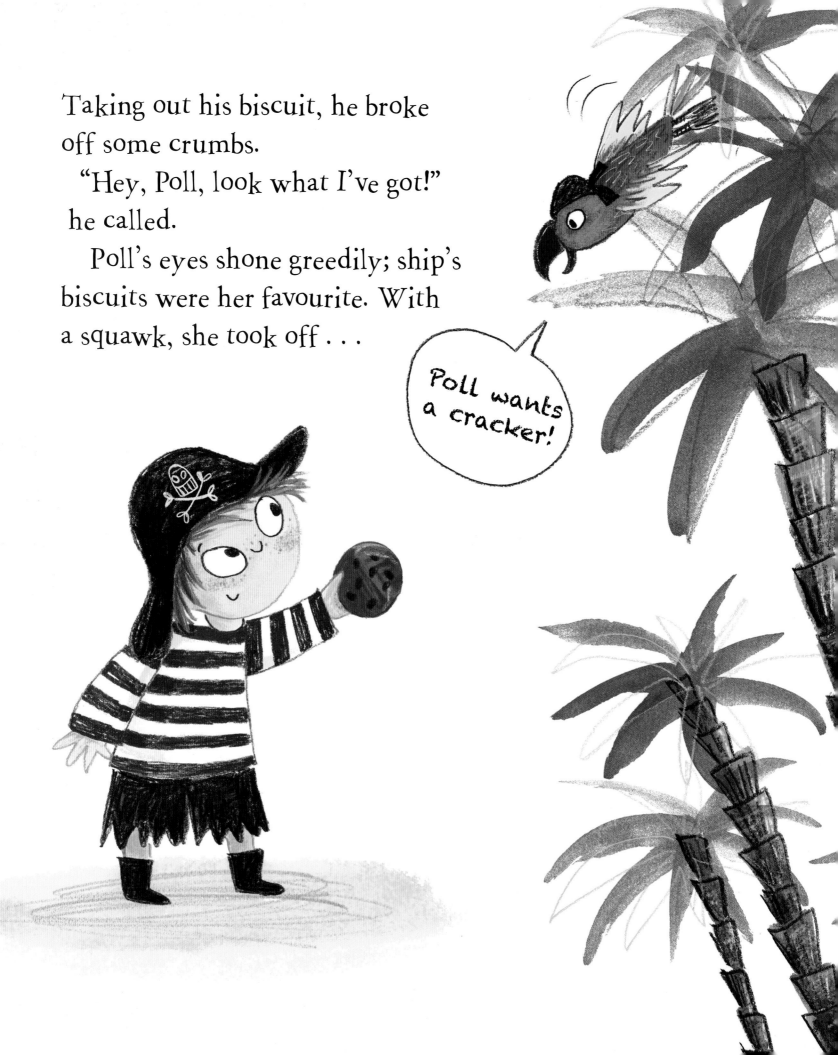

Taking out his biscuit, he broke off some crumbs.

"Hey, Poll, look what I've got!" he called.

Poll's eyes shone greedily; ship's biscuits were her favourite. With a squawk, she took off . . .

Poll wants a cracker!

. . . and landed neatly on Jake's hand.
"Thank heavens!" sighed
Miss Cherry.
"HOORAY!" cheered the class.
"That pesky parrot came back!"

Who's a clever Poll then?

Jake knew he was in BIG trouble.
Pesky parrots were sure to be
against the rotten rules.
   Miss Cherry folded her arms.
"Well, Jake, what should we do now?"
"Send me home?" mumbled Jake.

Miss Cherry laughed. "I've got a much better idea. Who likes singing?"

"ME!" shouted Jake, because singing is one thing pirates love best.

"Pots and brushes out, time to do some painting!" said Miss Cherry. "Follow me, mates!" cried Jake, because pirates love to make a sploshy mess.

By story time, Jake had forgotten his worries about the rotten rules and getting into trouble. He listened to Miss Cherry read a tale about treasure buried deep on Parrot Island. Even Poll seemed to like it.

At home time, Jake's family stood waiting at the gates.
"Well, lad?" they said.
"Was school hard and horrible?"
"NO!" cried Jake.
"I WANT TO GO AGAIN!"

And he told them all about his day.
"Well boil me bedsocks!" cried Pa.

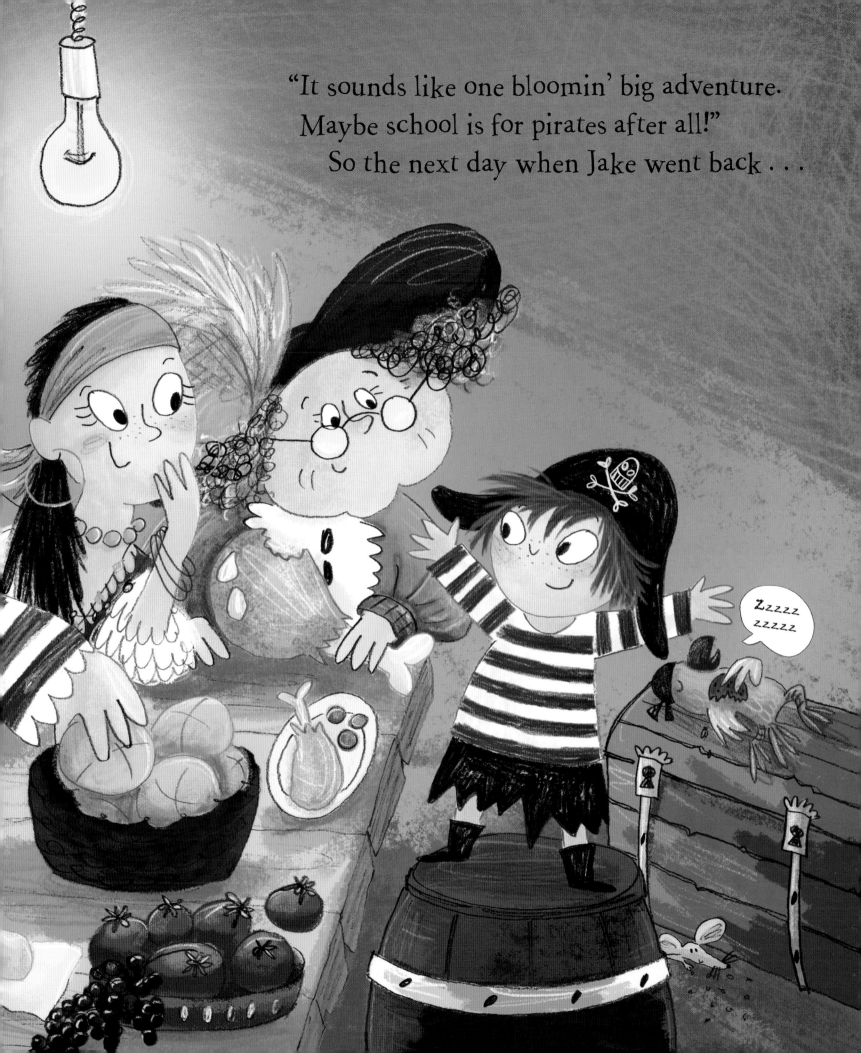

"It sounds like one bloomin' big adventure.
Maybe school is for pirates after all!"
So the next day when Jake went back . . .

Zzzzz
zzzzz

. . . he brought along his
whole bloomin' family!

More big adventures for
LITTLE PIRATES!

The Curious Case of the Missing Mammoth
Ellie Hattie · Karl James Mountford

Tracey Corderoy · Tony Neal
THE ONE-STOP STORY SHOP

Steve Smallman
ITCHY SCRITCHY SCRATCHY PANTS
Elina Ellis

PIRATES in PYJAMAS
CAROLINE CROWE · TOM KNIGHT

The SPACE TRAIN
Maudie Powell-Tuck · Karl James Mountford

SHHH! I'M READING!
JOHN KELLY · ELINA ELLIS

LiTTLE TiGER

For information regarding any of the above titles or for our catalogue, please contact us:
Little Tiger Press Ltd, 1 Coda Studios, 189 Munster Road, London SW6 6AW
Tel: 020 7385 6333 • E-mail: contact@littletiger.co.uk • www.littletiger.co.uk